MW00903196

Angel scurried off and bumped into her cousin in the hallway. "Where are you off to in such a hurry?" asked Jaida. "I was coming to look for you," Angel replied. Angel then paused and stood with a troubled look on her face. "What's wrong Angel?" Jaida asked. "Why do you think I have two mommies?" Angel asked. "I think you have two mommies, because if one mom says no to something you can go ask your other mom," said Jaida. Angel started laughing. "Hey, don't laugh, it works every time for me with my mommy and daddy; you should try it," said Jaida. Continuing Jaida explained, "You have two mommies because they met and fell in love and wanted to have children together, just like my parents. At least that is what my daddy says," replied Jaida. Angel smiled from ear to ear, she thought to herself, "My mommies must really love me." "Thanks Jaida," Angel said. Then they both ran towards the living room.

In the kitchen, Grandma was preparing her famous raisin bread. Angel thought to herself, "Hmm, I bet grandma will know why I have two mommies." "Hi Grandma," Angel said as she sat down at the kitchen table. "Hello there Angel," replied her Grandma. The little girl sat with a puzzling look on her face. "Why so puzzled?" Grandma asked. Angel replied, "Grandma, can you tell me why I have two mommies and everyone else has a mommy and a daddy?" Stunned, Grandma dropped the box of raisins. As she began to pick up the fallen raisins, she answered, "Well Angel, you have two mommies because you are very special." "Well aren't the other kids special too?" Angel questioned. "Well every kid is special dear, you just have two mommies that both wanted you and love you dearly, and instead of only one getting you, they decided to share," Grandma replied softly. "I love to share my toys with my friends!" replied Angel. As Angel got up from the table she said, "Thanks Grandma." "You're welcome Angel. Now come back later and I'll share my famous raisin bread with you," said Grandma.

Angel climbed on her grandfather's lap and sat quietly. "Is everything ok?" he questioned. She looked up and said, "Grandpa I was wondering, why do I have two mommies?" Her grandfather was shocked as he was not expecting this question. He looked at her and said, "Well Angel, you have two mommies because two is better than one." "Why is two better than one?" she questioned with a confused glare. Grandpa handed a piece of candy to his granddaughter. She smiled brightly, he then handed her another piece of candy and she smiled even brighter. Grandpa then asked, "If you have two pieces of candy, it's better than one correct?" "Correct," she said smiling from ear to ear. She was excited to get candy and even more excited that her grandpa knew the answer to her question. "You're right, two is better than one," she said as she hopped off her grandfather's lap and headed towards the kitchen. As Angel approached the kitchen, Grandpa yelled out, "And remember no candy until after lunch Angel."

Angel headed down the stairs where she saw her grandpa reading the newspaper in the living room. "Good afternoon Grandpa," she said as she got closer to him. "Well, good afternoon Angel," he replied as he placed the newspaper down beside him.

One summer afternoon while visiting her grandparents, Angel woke up from her afternoon nap. The sun was beaming through the window and she heard children playing nearby. A voice yelled out "Mommy, mommy, when is daddy coming home?" Shortly after, another voice replied, "Very soon." As she sat in her bed and listened to the little girl talk to her mother, she thought to herself, "Why do I have two moms?" Angel always wondered why her family looked different. Perhaps, it was because all of her friends had a mommy and a daddy. She climbed out of bed and put on her purple rabbit-eared slippers and decided that she needed some answers.

To my beautiful daughter. I know that you
are always watching, so with everything
that I do, I do it for you. Thank you for
being my muse, my heart, my everything.
I dedicate this book to you...My Inspiration.

- Love Mom

www.twomommiesbook.com

twomommiesbook@gmail.com

Printed in the United States of America

First Printing, 2017

ISBN-13: 978-1546979692
ISBN-10: 1546979697

Why Do I Have Two Mommies?

"Papa, Papa, can we go outside to play?" asked Jaida. "Sure, I have to speak with grandma first and then we can all go outside," replied Grandpa. Excited, the girls head straight to the front door to put on their shoes. Goldie, grandpa's dog was hanging around by the front door ready to go outside. As Angel was putting on her shoes she said, "Goldie, do you know why I have two mommies?" "Ruff Ruff," Goldie barked in response and proceeded to lick the young girl's face. Jaida said, "Oh Angel, Goldie can't talk." The girls burst out in laughter. Grandpa finally finished speaking with Grandma and he and the girls head outside.

The girls grabbed their bikes from the shed on the side of the house. They quickly spotted their play buddy Miyoku, playing in the yard next door. Angel yelled out, "Hey Miyoku! Would you like to ride bikes with us?" "Sure," he replied. The children began to ride up and down the neighborhood street. Miyoku started to feel tired. "I need a break," he claimed. "Me too," Angel replied gasping for air. They placed their bikes down and took a seat in the yard. Jaida continued to ride, going up and down the street. "Look guys, no hands!" she yelled out. "How cool, no hands," said the young boy.

Angel began to play with a family of ants she saw in the yard. "There are so many ants," she remarked as she watched them go in and out of the ant hill. "I wonder which one is the mom and which one is the dad?" pondered Miyoku. "What if they have two mommies like I do?" Angel asked quickly. "They might even have two dads. Like my friend Christian at school," said Miyoku. Angel became quiet and sat with a baffled expression. "Is everything ok?" asked her friend. Angel looked up and asked, "Miyoku, do you know why I have two mommies?" "My dad says my mom has superpowers and that her kisses are magical. And you have two moms, so that makes double magical kisses," the young boy continued. "You're right my moms' kisses are pretty awesome and they always make me feel better," said Angel. "A yell from a distance, called out, "Miyoku it's time for lunch." "Hey! I've got to go Angel, that's my dad. See you later," said Miyoku. "Ok, see you later," Angel replied.

Angel could see the neighbor, Mr. Patel tending to his garden. She decided to approach him. "How are you today Mr. Patel?" "I'm great, thanks for asking. And how are you?" Mr. Patel asked. "I'm fine," she replied. Angel then stood lingering around, quietly watching her neighbor. "Angel do you like flowers?" he asked. "Yes, I love flowers," Angel replied. Angel once again stood really quiet. "Are you ok Angel?" Mr. Patel asked. She looked up and asked him the same question. "Do you know why I have two mommies?" He looked at her with a kind smile and proceeded to explain. "All families are different and unique. Some families have two dads and some kids have grandparents as parents. The great thing about that is that no matter what, you have two mommies who love you unconditionally." He went to pick a yellow and red rose and handed them to Angel. He then said, "I plant red and yellow roses together because it means joy, happiness, and excitement and that is what you bring to your mommies Angel." Beaming from ear to ear she said, "Oh thank you, thank you Mr. Patel. I'm going to give these to my mommies when they come to pick me up." "You're welcome Angel," Mr. Patel replied. "Talk to you later Mr. Patel," Angel said before running off to play.

"Angel saw Jaida playing in the yard with toys. "Jaida, Jaida look at what Mr. Patel gave me!" said Angel. Jaida admired the beautiful flowers. "How pretty!" "Mr. Patel said they mean joy and excited-ness," Angel said. "You mean joy and excitement," replied her cousin. "Yes and happiness," replied Angel. The girls laughed and continued playing with their toys. Shortly after, Grandpa yelled out, "Five more minutes girls." Jaida jumped up, "I'm going to spend five more minutes riding my skateboard."

Goldie, grandpa's dog was sunbathing in the yard. Angel collected all of her toys and walked over to pet him. "Goldie my family is unique like your family, you have grandma and grandpa," said Angel. "Ruff, Ruff," Goldie barked. "Time to come in girls," Grandpa yelled. The girls quickly dashed towards the house.

The doorbell rang. Grandpa opened the door and welcomed in both of Angel's mothers. Angel ran and rushed into their arms. "Well hello to you too Angel," said Mom. She grabbed both of her mothers' hands, pulling them into the living room. While they were taking a seat, she ran to the kitchen and brought back the flowers she'd gotten from Mr. Patel. "These are beautiful!" they responded. Their daughter overly excited began to explain, "They mean joy and excited and to be happy." "Slow down," says mommy. Angel took a deep breath and continued, "Mr. Patel said that yellow and red flowers mean joy and excitement and to be happy. And you know what else I learned today? I learned, why I have two mommies." The couple looked at each other in complete shock. Angel grabbed their hands and placed them together. "I have two mommies because two is better than one, and because I'm special, and because you fell in love, and because your kisses are awesome and because our family is unique." Mommy gently touched her little girl's hair and proudly replied, "Angel you have two moms because God trusted us to be your parents. And it's our responsibility to love you, protect you and guide you. We don't choose our unique families Angel, they are chosen for us." Both women pulled their daughter closer and gave her a heartfelt hug, together they said, "We love you Angel."

THE END

Made in the USA
Monee, IL
24 March 2021